THESEUS
—— AND THE ——
MINOTAUR

For Benjamin and Joseph — H. L. and D. M.

To Ruben and Mathis — C. H.

● ● ● ● ● ● ● ●

Pronunciation guide

Aegeus . . . . ee-GEE-us	labyrinth . . . . LAH-beh-rinth
Aegle . . . . AYE-glay	Minos . . . . MY-noss
Ariadne . . . . ah-REE-ad-nee	Minotaur . . . . MY-noh-tor
Asterius . . . . ast-AIR-ee-us	Mount Olympus . . . . MOUNT oh-LIM-pus
Athene . . . . ah-THEE-nee	Naxos . . . . NACKS-oss
Corona Borealis . . . . . . coh-ROH-nah boh-ree-AL-iss	Pasiphae . . . . pah-SIFF-aye
Crete . . . . KREET	Talos . . . . TAH-loss
Daedalus . . . . DYE-dull-us	Theseus . . . . THEE-see-us
Dionysus . . . . DYE-oh-nice-us	tyrant . . . . TIE-rant
Icarus . . . . ICK-ar-us	

● ● ● ● ● ● ● ●

Bibliography

Graves, Robert. *The Greek Myths*. London: Pelican, 1955.
March, Jenny. *Cassell's Dictionary of Classical Mythology*. London: Cassell Reference, 1998.
Ovid. *Metamorphoses*. Translated by Mary Innes. London: Penguin, 1955.

● ● ● ● ● ● ● ●

Barefoot Books
2067 Massachusetts Ave
Cambridge, MA 02140

Text copyright © 2013 by Hugh Lupton
  and Daniel Morden
Illustrations copyright © 2013 by Carole Hénaff
The moral rights of Hugh Lupton, Daniel
  Morden and Carole Hénaff have been asserted

First published in the United States of America
  by Barefoot Books, Inc in 2013
All rights reserved

Graphic design by Ryan Scheife,
  Mayfly Design, Minneapolis, MN
Color separation by B & P International,
  Hong Kong
Printed in China on 100% acid-free paper
This book was typeset in Agamemnon,
  Dante MT Std and Mynaruse
The illustrations were prepared in acrylics

ISBN 978-1-84686-782-8

Library of Congress Cataloging-in-Publication
  Data is available under LCCN 2012035706

1 3 5 7 9 8 6 4 2

THESEUS
AND THE
MINOTAUR

RETOLD BY HUGH LUPTON & DANIEL MORDEN

ILLUSTRATED BY CAROLE HÉNAFF

Barefoot Books
step inside a story

CONTENTS

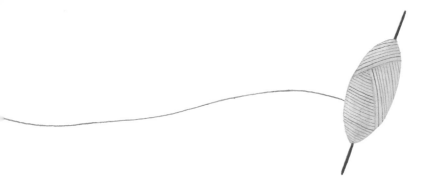

CHAPTER ONE

THE JEALOUS UNCLE

I MAGINE A TYRANT. IMAGINE a king so powerful, so fearsome, that other kings from all over the world sent him ships laden with treasures and tributes each month to appease him. Minos of Crete was such a king.

One of the kings who sent him treasure was the ruler of a city far away to the north, King Aegeus of Athens.

Owl-eyed Athene, the goddess of war and wisdom, loved the city of Athens. She loved the people of Athens. Most of all she loved people who were like her — quick and clever, crafty and cunning.

She was particularly fond of an inventor called Daedalus. He had made a sword so sharp that it never struck in battle without killing its victim. He had made a room in the root of a volcano that was warm in the coldest of winters. He had made a honeycomb out of gold that was so lifelike that bees would crawl across it searching for sweetness.

But the one Athene loved most was Daedalus's nephew, Talos. He was the cleverest of them all. When he was eight he had invented the first maze, a labyrinth for his pet rat. When he was ten he had invented the first kite, made from the feathers of a bird. Now he was twelve, and he was sitting with his uncle eating fish stew in their home high above the sea. When the stew was finished he reached into his bowl and pulled out a fish's jawbone. He felt the row of sharp teeth with the tip of his finger. Suddenly he smiled to himself and dropped the bone.

Daedalus watched the boy. He wondered what was running through his mind.

The next morning Daedalus woke up to hear a strange rasping sound. Talos had fashioned the very first saw, with a row of bronze teeth like the teeth of a fish. He was cutting through a piece of wood.

Daedalus was filled with jealous rage — a bitter, yellow, bubbling, seething rage that he couldn't control. Why hadn't he thought of that himself? Mad with jealousy, he grabbed the boy by the scruff of the neck and hurled him over the edge of the cliff. Talos fell, flailing, plunging, tumbling through the air.

But nothing is hidden from the eyes of the mighty gods and goddesses. Athene saw

her favorite falling and came to his rescue. All at once, Talos felt feathers, black and white feathers, pushing out of his arms. He felt feathers pushing out of his body. He felt his lips hardening into a beak. He felt a plume of feathers bursting out of the top of his head. The goddess had turned him into a bird, a lapwing, the very first of its kind. Talos beat his feathered arms against the air and flew, a strange lifting, tumbling flight, never very far from the ground. For the lapwing is the only bird afraid of heights — Talos has never forgotten his terrible fall.

CHAPTER TWO

THE INVENTOR'S CHALLENGE

WHEN KING AEGEUS HEARD that Daedalus had tried to murder his nephew, he sent soldiers to seize him so that he could be punished for his crime. But Daedalus was too quick for them and made his escape. He climbed onto a boat that was sailing south to Crete.

King Minos and his queen, Pasiphae, welcomed the famous inventor. Daedalus brought them gifts. To Minos he gave a bronze

map of his island kingdom: every hill, every river was etched into the shining surface. To Queen Pasiphae he gave a jointed statue, the perfect likeness of a human being, which could be moved into any posture. To their daughter, Princess Ariadne, he gave a golden crown. It was made of pure gold, and with a single spark from striking one stone against another, it could be set aflame, filling even the darkest of nights with brightness. Very quickly Daedalus became the favorite of King Minos.

One night he was summoned to the king's private chambers.

"It must seem to you that I want for nothing," said Minos. "I am rich. I have a fleet of ships that strikes terror into the hearts of countless kings. But the gods are cruel! The one thing they deny me is a son. What is the point of an empire without an heir? You above all other mortals are a maker of solutions. Make me a solution. Make me a son, and in return I will make you rich!"

Daedalus bowed his head and set to work. He made a solution: a potion that Queen Pasiphae had to drink on a special night when the moon was in the constellation of the bull. Queen Pasiphae became pregnant. Minos was overjoyed. He showered gifts on Daedalus.

"It is a son! I know it is a son. What name shall we give him?" the king asked Pasiphae.

"It is thanks to the stars that he came to us. We should thank the stars for him," she replied.

So they agreed the child would be called Asterius, which means "of the stars."

CHAPTER THREE

A CHILD IS BORN

THE DAYS TURNED TO WEEKS.
The weeks turned to months. After five
months, Pasiphae was huge with child. Six,
seven, eight months — she could no longer
walk. She took to her bed. After another month
she went into labor. Minos was fetched. He
sent away the midwives. He wanted to be the
first to lay eyes on his son...But when the baby
appeared, the king looked on in horror. The
child had the head and the horns of a bull!

"Fetch Daedalus!" cried Minos.

A servant brought Daedalus from his quarters. Minos pointed at his son with a trembling hand. "Look at it! Look what you've done! Get rid of it!"

"No!" exclaimed Pasiphae. "You will not kill my child!"

Daedalus looked from raving king to sobbing queen. Somehow he had to please them both.

"Great king, I have a solution. I'll make a prison for him — a secure place from which he will never escape."

In the caves beneath the palace, Daedalus set to work. Remembering the maze his nephew Talos had made for his pet rat, he constructed a labyrinth. It was a labyrinth of such complexity that if any human being — apart from its maker — took three steps into it they would become utterly lost. In the center of the maze he hollowed out a chamber. A chute was dug from the palace above, down which food and drink could be lowered.

One night, while horn-headed Asterius was fast asleep, Daedalus took him in his arms and carried him into the maze. He placed him in the central chamber and slipped away.

Up above, Queen Pasiphae stood at the top of the chute. She heard her son wake, and cry for his mother — he cried and cried, while she stood helpless in the room above. But he did not die. He ate the food and drink that were lowered down to him. Down in the dark maze beneath the palace, Asterius was growing bigger and stronger by the day.

CHAPTER FOUR

A MONSTER IS BORN

THE DAYS TURNED TO WEEKS. The weeks turned to months. The months turned to years. Fifteen years went by. Queen Pasiphae went to her husband.

"It is so long since we heard anything from... below," she said. "I'm afraid he may be dead."

Minos sent a human chain into the labyrinth, a chain of servants holding hands so that they would not get lost in the twisting tunnels of the maze. The king and queen stood at the top of the chute. They heard sniffing... shouts of alarm...

bellowing...shouting...ripping...screaming...
tearing...chewing...and then silence.

Daedalus crept into the maze to see what
had happened. When he returned he reported
to Minos, "He ate them, your highness. Why
shouldn't he? He has been given the flesh of

cows to eat. No one has told him it is wrong to eat the flesh of men and women."

From then on Asterius refused all other food. He threw himself against the walls of his prison. He snorted and roared. There was no peace in the palace. Not even Minos could listen to the sound of his hungry son, bellowing for food and dying for lack of it. So he sent seven young men into the maze. Then another seven. Only young men were sent in, for Minos hated the sight of them. Whenever he saw one he was reminded of his own son, that thing of shame skulking in the shadows.

Daedalus shuddered. He had a secret son, whose mother was a Cretan slave girl. He was a beautiful, golden-haired boy called Icarus. Daedalus knew that if Minos learned of the boy's existence he would be filled with jealousy and send him to a horrible death. So he kept Icarus hidden in a secret chamber in his private quarters.

But soon there were no longer enough young men left on Crete to feed the monster. So Daedalus went to Minos and said, "The neighboring kingdoms all fear you. What if you were to demand that each kingdom send seven young men a year in tribute? Asterius would never want for food again."

CHAPTER FIVE

THE KING'S SACRIFICE

A ND SO THE DECREE WENT out. Each kingdom sent seven young men: seven young men who would never be heard of again. Rumors traveled from Crete with trading ships, rumors of a flesh-eating beast beneath Minos's palace called the Minotaur.

Soon it was Athens's turn. But King Aegeus resisted, unable to bring himself to send seven young Athenians to a horrible death. Furious, Minos ordered a fleet of ships to sail to Athens with himself in command.

The people of Athens watched the ships slicing through the waves toward them. Every man, woman and child looked on in fear. As soon as the ships reached the quayside, King Minos and his soldiers leapt ashore. They marched through the streets of Athens and wherever they saw a young man of noble bearing King Minos would shout, "Seize him!"

Six young men had been taken by the time they had reached the palace of King Aegeus. Standing behind the king's throne was a youth with a crown of laurel leaves on his head. He looked like a god. He could almost have been Ares, the beautiful god of war. Minos shouted: "He will be the seventh!"

King Aegeus fell to the ground at Minos's feet. "Please!" he cried. "He is my own son, my only son, Theseus. I beg you, spare his life."

Minos kicked Aegeus aside. "Seize the prince!" he commanded.

But before the soldiers could grab him, Theseus stepped forward. "No need to bind my arms," he said. "I come happily, of my own free will. I look forward to meeting your Minotaur."

The seven Athenian youths boarded an Athenian ship. It was a ship with black sails, because everyone believed that they were sailing to their deaths.

The next morning King Aegeus went down to the quayside, accompanied by a beautiful young Athenian woman called Aegle. Aegle saw Theseus leaning over the rail of the ship. She threw her arms around his neck. "Theseus, you will not forget me, will you?" she cried.

"Aegle, I will never forget you, and when I return I will make you a queen of Athens."

Then King Aegeus spoke to his son, "Theseus, if you die it will break my heart. But if, by the grace of the mighty gods, you return safely home to Athens, please, I beg you, swap these black sails for white ones, so that I may know the best or the worst before any word reaches me."

Theseus bowed his head. "Father, I promise. I will do so," he said.

Then the ropes were untied and the black-sailed ship left the harbor, surrounded by the white-sailed ships of King Minos.

CHAPTER SIX

LOVE IN A DANGEROUS TIME

FOR THREE DAYS AND THREE nights they sailed. When they reached the island of Crete there was a blaring of horns and trumpets to greet the king on his return. The seven Athenian youths were led to the palace in a glittering procession. They were invited to sit down to a feast. But as they tasted the savory meats and sipped the sweet wines, they could hear the sound of keys turning in locks. They knew that they were trapped.

They slept that night between silken sheets and beneath purple blankets. But the next morning there were only six of them at the breakfast table. As they ate they heard the distant sound of screaming from somewhere far below. Five pushed their plates away, but Theseus chewed his food and listened.

King Minos entertained his guests. They were invited to compete with the finest Cretan runners, leapers, wrestlers and archers. Theseus defeated them all. In the evenings, Princess Ariadne would dance for them, her blazing crown upon her head, making the shadows of the great hall leap around her.

So the days went by. Then, one morning, there were five of them at the breakfast table. Then there were four.

Ariadne could not take her eyes off Theseus. When he was running or wrestling,

she would be watching him. When she was dancing, her eyes were fixed on him. Theseus felt the weight of her gaze and smiled to himself.

Then there were three of them at the breakfast table. Then two.

When no one was watching, Theseus seized Ariadne by the hand. "Ariadne, from the moment I first saw you I have loved you. I could have made you so happy. I could have taken you to Athens. I could have made you a queen."

She looked at him and tears spilled down her cheeks. Then, shaking her head, she pulled her hand away and ran from the room.

One morning, Theseus found that he was alone at the breakfast table. He waited for his chance and then approached the princess again.

"Ariadne, is there nobody who can help me?" he said. "If I could escape, I would take you with me."

Ariadne could not help herself. She melted into his arms, pressing her lips to his. "Yes, yes, there is someone . . ." Then, breaking from his embrace, she ran to find Daedalus.

CHAPTER SEVEN

A CUNNING PLAN

"**I** WANT YOU TO HELP THIS Theseus defeat my brother," Ariadne said to Daedalus.

Daedalus shook his head. "I cannot," he replied. "Your father would be furious with me."

"You must. If you don't, I will tell my father about your secret son. Oh yes, I have seen what my parents have not. I have seen young Icarus. And when my father lays eyes on your boy, you know as well as I what will happen. Icarus will be sent into the maze to be devoured. So you have no choice but to help Theseus!"

Daedalus bowed his head and set to work. That night he slipped out of the palace and placed inside the entrance to the maze the things Theseus would need to defeat the monster.

Meanwhile, Ariadne crept into Theseus's gilded bedchamber. Leaning over the bed, she whispered, "My love, when they take you to the labyrinth, feel among the shadows to your left. You will find my crown to light your way. You will find a ball of golden thread so that you won't get lost. And you will find a bronze sword . . . for my brother. When you have finished, wait by the entrance of the labyrinth until nightfall and I will meet you outside." She kissed him and slipped away.

The next morning, King Minos was amazed. Theseus emerged from his bedchamber

of his own free will. There was no need to drag him from his room screaming and shouting. Surely by now he understood his fate? Why was he so relaxed — chatting to the guards and cracking jokes?

Down to the maze they went. Theseus was shown to the entrance of the labyrinth. He stepped inside. The darkness swallowed him, and there was silence.

CHAPTER EIGHT

INTO THE LABYRINTH

JUST AS ARIADNE HAD TOLD HIM,
Theseus felt among the shadows to his left.
His fingers closed around her crown and he
lifted it onto his head. He felt for the two stones
and struck them together. The crown blazed
with light. He found the ball of golden thread
and tied the end to a snag of rock. Picking up
the bronze sword, he began to make his way
into the labyrinth. He followed the tunnels
as they forked right and left, unraveling the
thread as he went. Above his head the shadows

danced. Beneath his feet were shreds of rag and splinters of bone picked clean.

Suddenly, he could hear the creature, grunting and snorting. Then he could smell it: the sour smell of sweat mingling with the sickly sweet stench of rotten flesh. Then he saw it: the human body, the great bull's head — the Minotaur.

Asterius had never seen such brightness before. Ariadne's crown blazed with light, and the he was filled with terror. He lurched and lost his balance, blinded.

Theseus laughed. This was easy! He plunged his sword into the beast's belly.

Asterius, still reeling in the bright light, felt something pierce his skin. He screamed . . .

Up above, Minos heard the screaming. That was a human sound. A human was dying, not a monster. Theseus was dead!

Again and again, Theseus stabbed the Minotaur. He stabbed its neck, its arms, its thighs, its chest. He opened up a constellation of wounds. The beast sank to its knees. Theseus seized it by one of its horns and hacked off its head.

Dragging the head in one hand and winding in the golden thread with the other, he made his way back through the tunnels as they twisted to the right and to the left. At last he saw the entrance to the labyrinth. He crouched down and waited until nightfall.

When the stars began to shine in the sky above, Theseus emerged from the labyrinth. Ariadne was waiting for him. He lifted the great bull's head, the head of her brother, and thrust it onto a stake at the entrance to the maze. Then he seized Ariadne by the hand and they ran to the harbor, where the Athenian ship was still moored. They jumped onto the deck of the

ship and Theseus ordered the crew to cut the
ropes. Before they left the harbor they set fire
to all the Cretan ships, so that a black pall of
smoke rose into the sky, extinguishing the light
of the stars. Then they sailed away.

CHAPTER NINE

DAEDALUS PAYS
THE PRICE

"YOUR HIGHNESSES MUST come at once!" a servant cried.

King Minos and Queen Pasiphae looked out and saw smoke rising from the harbor. They went to their daughter's bedchamber... her bed was empty! They rushed to the maze to find the dripping head of Asterius on a stake. Minos ground his teeth. Pasiphae cradled the head of her son and wept bitter tears.

Soldiers were sent to the chambers of Daedalus. They found him with a young man. They were so alike that the boy had to be Daedalus's son. Both of them were dragged before the king.

"Look where all your cleverness has brought us!" cried Minos. "My fleet is at the bottom of the harbor, and my daughter has fled with that Athenian trickster Theseus! You will pay for this."

"Your highness, I beg you," pleaded Daedalus. "Please don't put us into that dark place below!"

The king grinned. "You will rot in this maze of your own making," he replied.

Daedalus and Icarus were slung into the labyrinth. Daedalus reached up to a secret ledge. He had hidden an oil lamp and some other supplies there. He lit the lamp and set to work.

A pigeon was nesting in a crevice. He caught it and stretched out its left wing. Taking the furthermost feather between finger and thumb, he pulled. The bird shrieked and flew up. Daedalus snatched it from the air. He stretched out the right wing. He took the furthermost feather between finger and thumb and pulled. Each time he removed a feather he studied the bird's attempts at flight... and he learned much.

Icarus watched, fascinated. He saw a fluffy feather at his feet. He picked it up and blew. It lifted at the command of his breath... then fell.

CHAPTER TEN

LOVE BETRAYED

ARIADNE AND THESEUS sailed towards Athens. Ariadne had never been so happy. There was a fair wind, and after two days they came to the island of Naxos. Theseus suggested they go ashore for fresh meat and fruit. That night they lit a fire on the beach. They ate, they talked, they laughed, they danced. Then they slept in the warmth of the fire.

In the middle of the night, Ariadne woke. She was alone. She sat up and looked about. By the light of the moon she could see the

Athenian ship. She could see the anchor being lifted and the sails being unfurled. She ran down to the water's edge. "Theseus!" she cried.

From the deck of the ship came the sound of mocking laughter. There was a thud at her feet, then another, then a third. Looking down, she saw her crown, the ball of golden thread and the bronze sword lying on the sand. The wind filled the sails, the prow of the ship sliced through the waves, and Theseus was gone. He had vanished into the night.

Ariadne dropped to her knees, buried her face in her hands and trembled with sobs.

But nothing is hidden from the mighty gods. Dionysus, the god of drinking and drunkenness, of madness and ecstasy, of wild dancing and wild music, saw her and felt pity stirring in his heart. He came down from the heavens and lifted her to her feet.

"Ariadne," he said, "Theseus might have broken his promise to make you a queen of Athens... but I will make a promise that I will keep. I will make you a queen of the heavens."

He took her crown and set it in the sky as the constellation Corona Borealis. Then he led her up to the high slopes of Mount Olympus where she became his consort, his queen.

Theseus sailed homeward. All day he sailed. And as the sun was sinking, he saw the city of Athens ahead of him. He saw people standing on the cliff tops looking out to sea. He scanned the cliffs, sheltering his eyes from the sun. Was Aegle there waiting for him, and perhaps his father too?

Then suddenly he saw a figure falling, flailing, plunging from cliff to sea. Who could it be? He looked up and his heart sank. He had forgotten to swap the black sails for white ones.

His father, King Aegeus, thinking his son was dead, had hurled himself to his death.

Soon Theseus could see his father's broken body bobbing in the waves. With a boat hook, he lifted him onto the deck of the ship. He knelt beside the dripping corpse of Aegeus. And for the first time in his life, Theseus knew sorrow.

And ever since then, that body of water has been known as the Aegean Sea.

CHAPTER ELEVEN

ICARUS FLIES

I N CRETE, DAEDALUS HAD ONCE
again bent nature to his will. With the
bones of the dead, beeswax, feathers and linen
thread, he had made two pairs of wonderful
wings, one pair for himself and one for Icarus.

One night, just before dawn, Daedalus
woke Icarus and whispered urgently to him.
"Listen to me, my son," he said. "Minos controls
both land and sea, but he cannot control the
air. You and I will fly to freedom. It is still dark,

but follow me. When day breaks, you must remember this: if you fly too high, the heat of the sun will melt the wax that binds feather to bone. If you fly too low, the waves will splash against your wings and their sodden weight will drag you down. Follow me and ride the gusts I ride."

They went outside. The sky was filled with stars. No soldiers guarded the entrance to the labyrinth. There was no need — Minos controlled both land and sea. Under cover of darkness, Daedalus and Icarus made their way to the top of a cliff. They strapped on the wings. They embraced. Then they ran to the cliff edge and leapt, beating their feathered arms against the air...

They rose! They rose into the cool night sky! Every surging gust of wind made Icarus cry out with joy. All his life he had hidden in dusty corners for fear of King Minos. Now the sweep of the broad sky was above him, and the dark sea beneath! He saw a band of red ahead. Day was coming. Island after island passed by beneath, some no more than barren rocks jutting out of the sea, some much bigger and dotted with farms and villages. Icarus laughed at the little figures as they shouted and pointed far below. Higher he flew, and higher again.

A gust of wind lifted him. He lurched. A feather fell. He looked up to see the bird that had shed it, but his gaze met only the fierce eye of the hot sun. A shower of feathers was fluttering down now...

Daedalus turned to look back. Icarus was no longer following him, but tumbling, flailing, screaming as he plunged headlong into the sea.

In desperation, Daedalus flew to the nearest island and found a fishing boat. He

rowed out across the water and retrieved the corpse of his son.

His hot tears splashed against the boy's face, and for the first time, Daedalus knew sorrow.

And ever since then, that body of water has been known as the Icarian Sea.

In the burial grounds of the city of Athens, a son said farewell to his father. As Theseus walked away from the grave of old Aegeus, he was aware of a strange light blazing high overhead. He looked up. There was a new constellation in the sky, a circlet of mocking stars — Ariadne's shining crown.

Meanwhile, on a small island, a father buried his son. As Daedalus dug the grave, he too glimpsed something in the sky. He looked up to see a black and white bird rising and plunging. Every time the bird plummeted,

Daedalus thought of his son and sobbed. Then he remembered another falling boy. He remembered Talos, whom he had pushed from a cliff in Athens.

Daedalus watched the lapwing mocking him, and he wept.

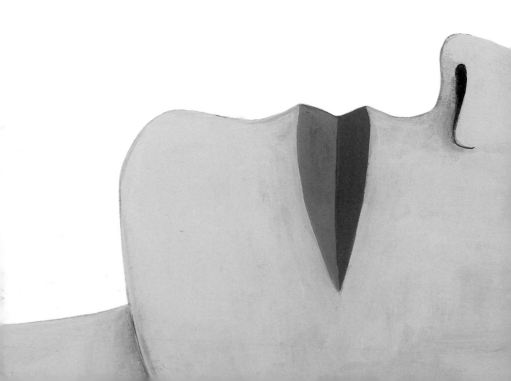

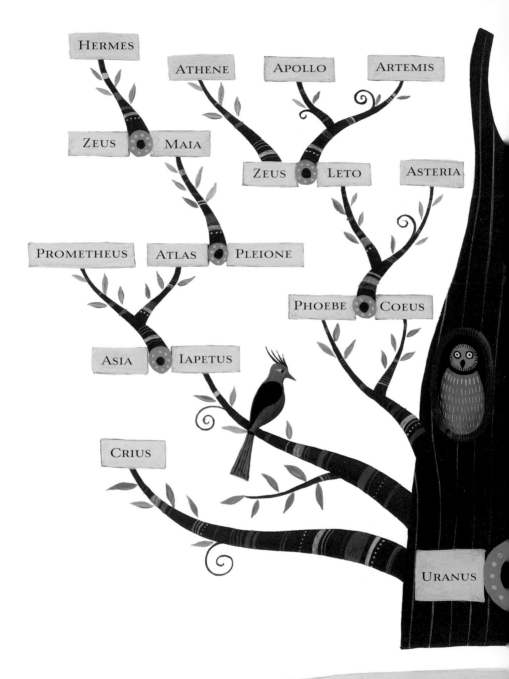

HERMES

ATHENE   APOLLO   ARTEMIS

ZEUS   MAIA

ZEUS   LETO   ASTERIA

PROMETHEUS   ATLAS   PLEIONE

PHOEBE   COEUS

ASIA   IAPETUS

CRIUS

URANUS

FAMILY TREE O

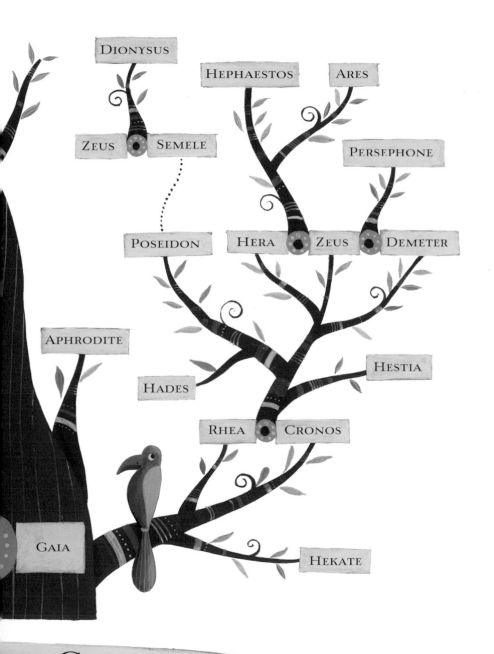

DIONYSUS

HEPHAESTOS   ARES

ZEUS   SEMELE   PERSEPHONE

POSEIDON   HERA   ZEUS   DEMETER

APHRODITE   HESTIA

HADES

RHEA   CRONOS

GAIA   HEKATE

HE GREEK GODS

ZEUS
GOD OF THUNDER

HERA
GODDESS OF MARRIAGE

APHRODITE
GODDESS OF LOVE

POSEIDON
GOD OF THE SEA

APOLLO
GOD OF THE SUN

ATHENE
GODDESS OF WISDOM

OLYMPIANS

DIONYSUS
GOD OF WINE

ARTEMIS
GODDESS OF THE HUNT

DEMETER
GODDESS OF THE HARVEST

ARES
GOD OF WAR

HEPHAESTOS
GOD OF FIRE

HERMES
MESSENGER GOD

THE ANCIENT GREEK WORLD

W

S

N

E

ITHACA

THESSALY

MACEDONIA

OLYMPIA

PELOPONNESE

ARCADIA

DELPHI

THEBES

ELEUSIS

MOUNT OLYMPUS

IOLCOS

LEMNOS

THRACE

SPARTA

MYCENAE

CORINTH

ATHENS

ATTICA

Aegean Sea

LESBOS

TROY

Mediterranean Sea

CRETE

Knossos

NAXOS

Icarian Sea

ASIA MINOR

Black Sea

CYPRUS